A Friend

D1743197

A Poem

I stood alone
Most of the year.

Not even birds
Would dare come near.

But when the snow

Lay on the ground,

Some children came
To play around.

When evening came
They all went home –

Except for one,
Left on his own.

I had a friend
For one whole night,
But then he melted
Out of sight.